The Error
In Our Ways

Poems By Eric Jordan Campbell

The Error In Our Ways

ISBN: 978-1729874455

Cover Art by Keiana Smith
Proofread by Eric Jordan Campbell
Edited by Eric Jordan Campbell

Eric Jordan Campbell

the error in our ways

to my brothers
Drew Tyler Campbell
Ryan Jalen Campbell
whether the light is blinding
or it is too dark to see your nose
we are in this together

to my parents
Sean Campbell and Leah Campbell
I am still trying to prove
to you
you made the right decisions.

the error in our ways

Eric Jordan Campbell

It is damn near impossible to understand the world
If you haven't yet left your birthplace.

Eric Jordan Campbell

Urban Turban

Through this lens I see an array of rainbows.
Magnificently magnified by beautiful auras.
I've learned changing angles changes scenery
So I hope you see the angels outnumber the demons
in me.
I pray your lens is wide enough to capture both the
human
and their religious beliefs.

Drugs You Should Try

I meant every word I ever said to you.
Every
single
one.
My sentences never had punctuation because I'm not
a fan of putting an end to something that isn't over
yet; that's why semicolons exist. When we spoke,
every breath I inhaled had the effects of opium and
every breath I exhaled screamed "I love you"

Constructing & Deconstructing

When you step back
and take a look at the house you've built,
is it something you can say you're proud of?

The Masquerade Ball Is Over

You jammed these words under my tongue
then ordered my mouth shut
how are you surprised
that this is the first thing I spit out

So often,
you've forced me to swallow my pain
so forgive me for flashing a smile
when I regurgitate upon your pretty clothes
they were only masking the ugliness inside you

our eyes connected when the clocks held hands
and neither of us could foresee
what was to come.
the only thing I knew to be true in that moment
was you.

I cannot tell you of your demons,

If I am too afraid to expose my own.

Who are you lying to?
Is it yourself?
What are you scared of?
Reaching out for help?
When is the last time you've been happy?
Even briefly.
When is the last time you didn't worry too much
When is the last time you enjoyed life?

ARE YOU LISTENING

Too often
we neglect
to weigh
how much our youth
has to do with our truth
so many tortured souls
forgotten missing children
dealing with pain
they wish would kill them

SHADOWS ARE ALWAYS WITH US, RIGHT?

it feels like
like sadness is hugging me
and tears are the only thing keeping me company
my only friend is the darkness

- but I fear it's consuming me.

You are a queen amongst peasants and I can't even
fathom how you breathe the same air as us
knowing that I romanticize the idea of love,
I don't think it's fitting to say I love you.
I adore you.
your quirks
mannerisms that make me roll my eyes
and smile
all in the same gesture.

THERAPIST

Neither of us know who owns the bed we lie in.
but that's not our concern
amidst the constant music
and joyous bodies
outside that locked door.
As you lie on this bed I see the whole world
I see mountains that I've moved just ten minutes ago
I see a valley that rises and falls
Small puddles and lakes all over your globe
Two hills that no man has ever seen previously
And rivers ever flowing from your eyes until they
meet the edge of the earth
And I ask what's wrong as I attempt to be your
therapist
But if I split that word in two I'd find my true calling...

WHEN YOUR ACTIONS SPEAK WHAT DO THEY SAY?

we have had enough conversations
where are the actual acts of love
just because you close your eyes
doesn't mean you didn't witness
the screams
the wails
the children being forced to watch their parents
tongues ripped from their mouths
Reminding them not to speak out of order

Tanks topple over buildings
you have room to offer them solace
you once wore your heart on your sleeve
and now tank tops are your everyday wear
You're out here sleeveless

Our story
Consisted of all things necessary for a story.
Freytag's Pyramid was followed precisely
Our story
Consisted of as little dialogue as possible.
Instead of ink
The words were written in drops of sweat.

We made love
You spoke in a foreign tongue
I responded with a tongue you knew well.

Fallen Sanctuaries

My sight was distorted when my eyes first opened
I rubbed trying to clear my view.
The vision shown to me was new.
As I watched my sanctuary turn to a place of business.
And I could no longer see the difference
Between the politics and religion.
That moment hurt the most.

THE BELT LINE

I watched paint dry.
I watched the paint peel.
I quenched my thirst with lead water.
I stared into time and space
My mother's ring passed my gaze
And I saw diamonds wave.
I witnessed them dull.
"Remove that blank look from your face."
Now I focus on how she hits me with every syllable.
I
TOLD
YOU
NOT
TO...

Her voice trails off
Until she says my favorite phrase.
"This hurts me more than it hurts you."

We are done coddling grown men.

Teach your sons to dismiss their egos.

Boys will be boys will be boys will be boys will be boys

Until you raise them to be men.

Bestow upon them the same values and accountability placed on young women

EASY LIVING

How easy it is to forget.

When it doesn't affect you.

When the ones lost, weren't your loved ones.

How easy it is to forget when it wasn't your child on the receiving end.

When it wasn't your daughter shrieking for help as some man had his way with her.

Indirectly telling her, her body is for nothing but his pleasure.

How easy it is to forget when it wasn't you that missed the call that may have allowed you to talk your son down from that ledge.

How easy it is to forget when your mother makes it home, and you didn't even think to worry.

How easy it is to forget, when your father won't get mistaken for an immigrant.

It's easier to forget the horror when it isn't your family being torn apart.

You see how easy it is to forget, when it's not their sisters and brothers being left for dead.

You see how easy it is to forget, when the bodies don't look like you.

i've been searching for peace
but when I close my eyes and dream
i still get no relief

i keep my eyes open
because eyelids act as curtains
and it's dark enough inside
i could really use the light

the error in our ways

*Inhale *

You come back to me like the wind
After it's been knocked out of me
And if that was a deep inhale
The exhale was an abyss

Exhale

Don't Hush Me As If I Am A Child

Douse restrictions in gasoline and set fire to the
boundaries
We used to fake snore until he was sound asleep
To sweep up behind his mistakes
In attempts to keep up his facade of being great
•
But tables turned at the turn of the century
When we no longer had to live nightmares where we'd
jail our dreams
We met freedom
Became close friends with liberation
Being married, is not the pinnacle
Single at 30 is no longer a stigma,
But a celebration.
The difference between
Want
And
Need
He needs you more than you want him.

I am most thankful for rainy days.
Because after 100 days of clear skies,
you can forget to appreciate them.
My thoughts chase each other like twin brothers
wanting to play with everything that isn't theirs.
The clouds have been following me
and so I strip myself of this overpriced clothing I've
been hiding beneath.
Finally allow my soul to surface
lose myself in the storm
and find myself between heavy raindrops
The truth prevails.
I've been fighting tooth and nail
To hide my fears.
My anxiety is driven by being afraid to fail.
I give my all
and when it doesn't go my way
I claim I didn't try hard enough.
But I did. I left every piece of my soul out there.
And it was not enough.
I find myself succeeding when I put forth no effort.
And now...
100 days of rain have passed.
But the forecast calls for clear skies tomorrow.

AVIARY

You are a novel
A plethora or platter of qualities
You are composed of galaxies and universes
Do not allow yourself to be summed up into one
word.
Your story is more than a phrase
A page
A chapter
Remember the days you were chasing after
The person you have finally become

THE OCEAN IS A LOT PRETTIER WHEN YOU AREN'T
DROWNING IN THE MIDDLE OF IT.

SAFE TRAVELS

I never pack light,
Which makes unpacking that much more dreary.
I'm ready for the world.
The uphill battles and downhill travels.
My mother hugs me
With an air that this could be the last embrace.
She believes in me.
And yet I can read the trepidation in her face.

The Night We Met

The Night We Met. . .

We met somewhere between the crowd
Between the rhythm and soft notes
Below the stars and above the tide
Your voice carried though it wasn't that loud
And on this dark night I found hope
in the way the light danced off her eyes.

Before tonight every step forward found me 20 in
reverse.
And each verse of sad songs ended with another glass
The nights found me on my ass and showers became
scarce.
My friends became scared and I always replied with
        "it's alright."

But you reminded me rainy days are necessary for
flowers to bloom.

Your scent has escaped my mind
The touch of your lips seems unfamiliar.
Your place in my bed has been filled by another.
With each passing month my memory
of your blemishes has diminished.
I attempt to hold on to the moments we've spent
But it seems they're just as elusive as your scent.

EXHAUSTION

I'm tired.
I'm tired of love.
I'm tired of love that doesn't work.
I am exhausted.
I hate putting the work in just to watch it not work out.
I give my love
I give my heart
I give my all.
This energy is never replenished
I hate getting close and tying knots
Just to have to cut the rope in two
And it never cuts evenly, its frayed every single time
I hate making connections
just to watch us disconnect in seconds
We never speak again as if we weren't more than friends
and that's what pains me the most.
You probably still know my deepest secrets.
The goals I don't tell others just in case I fail.
The shit in life I try my best to suppress.
Yet we will never talk again.
That's odd to me...

WHEN THE SUN ROSE YOUR HAIR WAS INFLAMED IN EMBERS OF RED AND YELLOW.

YOU ONCE TOLD ME "BLACK IS BEAUTIFUL"

I RECENTLY LEARNED TO SEE A PRISM OF COLORS IN THE SKIN I WAS BORN INTO.

FLEETING

You are wasting your time fixing someone else
when you can be refurbishing yourself.
Go ahead and decorate your insides
to resemble the love you deserve to receive.

I send love to all the queens burying princes

A new era of lynchings

The princesses and queens captured

And blindfolded so they don't know their true stature

The kings in chains who couldn't free themselves

To show the queens they matter

Who in turn could teach the offspring

How to untie the knots and nooses they were handed

at birth

Little did I know
That in the middle of Little Italy
I'd find a mysterious woman plagued by misery
Yet, still exudes so much joy.
Excluding men who still acted as boys.
Inwardly protesting peacefully to protect her energy,
Then, enter me.
A perfect pessimist
not quite quintessential
Just aware that light is essential
and committed to consciously exerting energy where
it's required.

You made me forget
Rhythm
And
Rhyme

Formation and syllables
Keeping
Thought
Aligned

Learning from a queen
I
Got
In formation

This realist was ready to reenlist
With my miss I'll walk confidently through
all levels of our awaiting inferno

My morning coffee
You give me a reason to wake up,
But you make it that much harder to get out of bed

SHE TAINTED HER PERFECTION WITH MARKINGS
MY NAME WAS UNWORTHY OF THE MARQUEE.

How is it, the memories fade that quick?
I remembered you until my last sip.
may have had too much to drink
we had moments by the sink
all went down the drain.
I never even got your number
somehow now you're just a number.
unable to even envision how your hair falls.
I've been staring at walls hoping to see what's no
longer there.
You were the best night of my life
And possibly just another notch in my bedpost.

You can have this broken heart as a souvenir
It's in need of a few repairs.
And the motor needs to be replaced.
A couple scars and battle wounds can be erased.
Are you willing to put the work in?
You can say yes, but I won't know for certain
Pain built up after a couple years
Who knows if it was worth the tears.
I can't say it's in great condition.
But I can guarantee it's efficient
Can't see inside, the windows are tinted.
But flaws won't exist when it's finished
Don't treat it like the previous last owner.
If you want it then you've got it, it's not a loaner.
There's a strict no return policy
Because I don't need to hear apologies.

Replicating Art

This paper is my canvas.
These words, my paint.
Each letter dances,
while thoughts march in like saints.
I hold my brush,
but can't seem to keep steady.
No tears flow though,
I've sculpted a rugged levy.
Now these wrists seem too heavy
This weight is equal to that of an anvil.
Shove my face into an anthill
to numb the pain.
Put that picture in another frame...
I want to weave my web so intricate
to explain a love for life so infinite.
My deepest sentiments...

I'm a sinner
pleading for redemption.
My knees are weakening
I've been singing
the devils prayer
need to spend a weekend in.

WHEN THE FLOWERS WILT

Silence in the room
As tears run down the face of each individual
Not a single happy tune plays in a moment so difficult
Nothing but sighs and sobs
We look for consolation we might find in God

The years we've spent
The tears we've lent
The fears we've bent
The cheers we've sent

But the love, the love is given endlessly
Are memories I can hold onto until next time.

Rated R

We grew up on dark humor
We joked of death because it followed so closely
A group of black children playing hide and go seek
from drugs, guns, police, and adults who might harm
them.
I find it.. hilarious that black children can't watch
movies based on their own lives
It is because there is an understanding.
That the images can be damaging
The idea of being harassed at such a young age seems
absurd to the ones who don't have to live what's
portrayed on the screen.

THE SEA OF UNKNOWN

I think about it often.
I used to look out in any direction and see nothing but water.
I was alone.
I battled with my thoughts.
Enticed myself in the deepest conversations I've ever had.
Debated the whys of life.
I often searched for civilization so I could engage in conversation less daring and more menial
I yearned for hour-long discussions on sports and weather.
Ones I'd otherwise dread
How deep is this water?
Which way should I go?
Two choices.
Starve. Drown.
I sat there. Indecision. Learning from a teacher I never knew existed.
Alas, my savior came.
Saved me from me.
Because as all thinkers know, your mind is the scariest place to be.
And yet, I find myself indulging in this treacherous bliss.

you wanted vulnerability from me
and I dug within myself to give it to you
knowing it would leave me unsettled
I did it to prove I trusted you more than I feared
negative outcomes
you still left
and left me distraught

I knew this could happen
You promised it wouldn't.

Now I'm here in a bed of broken promises
The same one where everything was honest
It housed all of our arguments and makeups

-2017-

I tried to meet your needs with vulnerability
You kept presenting false pretense
and broken promises
a perfect pessimist
the pain you caused couldn't be cured with sedatives
I can't continue to open the same door
and pretend to be surprised at the mess behind it
and if I keep looking for love
outside of myself then I'll never find it
I wish you told me that the time was rented
you only gave me a percentage
you promised way more effort
There's a reason you were glowing
and my skin was dull
I never lied, I never cheated
my hold on what mattered never weakened
carried you with me every weekend
I know you paint me as the villain and that hurts the
worst
I only know because I overheard your words

I am looking into the eyes of the person who used to
be my entire world

And I see darkness

A never-ending sea of nothingness

We lost touch

I failed to assess the areas that were problematic for
her

I crowned myself king for being a decent man

And found myself dethroned and carried to the
gallows.

I wished to live forever
my dreams are always of death
on earth I float amongst the stars
but I can't get close
I witness from afar
the burnouts are beautiful
chaos
some collapse upon themselves
I just watch as people gravitate towards the darkness
all I can do is watch.

IGNORANCE IS BLISS

There are days where I despise being empathetic
days where I fully comprehend the
aforementioned title phrase
where emotions hit like tidal waves
and though I can swim to safety I'm suffocating
watching those around me drown
I can't fathom the pain in which your screams don't
make a sound
now I wish my eyes would focus on celebrities more
than they do refugees
I see bodies ripped to shreds for us to then say
Rest In Peace
but that doesn't make any damn sense.

I wish to apologize
for all the times
Where you pointed me in the right direction
And I still failed to find what I was looking for.

be so honest with me that I can

stand upon your word without

having to perform a balancing act

while juggling
your lies

Are you the kind of man you wish upon your future
daughter?
Or do you wish to not have daughters for fear of men
like you?

you call this place home
this family calls you a visitor behind your back
some are rude enough to say it to your face
the name calling never truly ceases
you're trying to make a dollar out of fifteen cents
they wish to change you and hide you between couch
cushions

GEORGIA

you pass by houses with mass amounts of land
and wonder
if your ancestors were enslaved there

the trees know your bloodline better than you do.

Hunters Refuge

I've listened to every love song imaginable.
fantasized about fatherhood and envisioned a family.

I've chased this dream and left a trail of ruins.
seldomly looking back to help the ones I've hurt
I've tried to love and failed.
but to love, is to be vulnerable
and vulnerability and I have never seen eye to eye.
I can't even let people in past a certain surface level.
but you, you could level me with your eyes.
you find the flaws I've masked in time
I focused on making my facade a perfect image
and you scrub the paint away
with no more than a stroke of your thumb.

Will you love me as gently as the butterfly lands?
Will you be patient in your descent upon me?
When I warned you that my last experience did not go
well did you take heed?
Or did you ignore the alarm for your own selfish
reasons of consumption?

I gave into you an almost eternal hold
you know the type
the type that allows you to burn my soul
you've touched parts of me that no one knows
I can't look back now
you can turn back clocks but it won't change the time.

You are in the process of self destructing.
You are breaking your hands and arms
Trying to hang onto someone who doesn't want you.
Breaking your back
Carrying relationships
That give you little in return.

I strengthened muscles for you
I did everything in my power to make it work out
I focused on the areas you needed me to
I gave my all and that's why it hurts now
Without you here I have no idea how to readjust.
I aligned my days so I could give you the energy
required.
And now here I am
At 6pm
With nothing to do because this is usually when you'd
call.
And at 10 I'm
bored out of my mind
because this is when
Your head would be on my chest
And we'd talk about our stresses
So when I'm asked how I'm doing,
I actually don't know...

You were the sun
And he the moon
Both light.
You sometimes shone too bright
At times he seemed closer than any night
Bigger brighter and no risk to take flight
The two of you are separate entities of equal
importance
Your complexity was rivaled by his calmness
You've hidden behind clouds
He's been absent some nights

What gave you the right to enter my life and turn
darkness to lights than shone too bright
Who gave you the right to turn my waves of emotions
into oceans we can travel

On sunny days I enjoy stepping into my backyard
Walking over to my fence
And peeking into your garden
It's beautiful.
I often wonder if you planned
To perfectly place these plants

I watch as you tend to your aloes and dracaenas
I'm enthralled by the love you have for your baby's
breaths and hydrangeas
The way you glow when you are near your sunflowers.

They surround you and lean into you
As if you are their mother
Goddess.
                                        I know better than to pick the roses
                                            not for fear of the thorns
                                                    but instead
                        so I can continue to watch the garden grow.

Don't let man made lights distract you from seeing stars.

THE PAIN MY MOTHER HID

My mother made sure to always see my outfit before I
stepped out of her front door
At times she would tell me to change my shirt because

"That doesn't go with those pants"

But she never actually cares about my fashion choices
She needed to know what I wore in case she ever
needed to identify my body

I have dressed myself
thinking I'd look good enough to impress you
and now I'm told
there are parts of the outfit you do not like.
my face reddens from embarrassment
but I am becoming undone for you.

if you should ever meet the peak
and become eerily aware of your own mortality.
I hope your reflection is one
you are proud of.
I hope you've managed to find
at least one of the earth's great wonders
and it leveled you.
man often finds himself destroying beauty that was
here before him
in attempts of owning it.
do not be the man so insecure of something
breathtaking that you demolish it.

THEY'LL CONVINCE YOU IT'S YOUR FAULT

what took all of five minutes
left a lifetime of pain
the bruises left scars that don't heal overnight
they don't heal over time
the tears disappear, they dry like sweat did
and left the body cold
this body lays there feeling hollow
the fan blades cut through once still air
delivering a chill that tenses up the spine
only the bones exist now
the body has been taken
tongue ripped from its home so it cannot regurgitate
the vile spit in
silence fills the void of that mouth
so every time they speak they shiver
words crashing into each trying to all come out at
once

Roses

Adaptation is often necessary to survive.
Evolve or die.
When I look at a rose I wonder if it always had thorns.
What environment must you have been in,
in order to have such a protective feature .
Protection from what exactly?
Roses are aesthetically pleasing for their vibrant
petals
Yet...

The thorns protect the stem because it understands
its beauty is not limited to just the petals.
I look at you and wonder who you've adapted for,
Why you sting like wasps in the summer every time
you start to allow me get close.

At a young age, roses and their thorns taught me
To abandon my natural male instincts of capturing
every single thing I thought was pretty and pleasing
to the eyes
We want to attain everything that's beautiful
Often not understanding that in this, we are
destroying the beauty we once loved.
So I love from afar and wonder who you've adapted
for.

REMINDER

There will be times in life where you give all you have to give. Where you dig and dig and give the contents of your soul, and it still won't be enough.

- *This is not your end.*

OF ROYAL BLOOD

Here I stand.
A King amongst widowed Queens
as the people beg
for someone to take reign and lead.
The other kings all chose war amongst each other
instead of love
This is the result.
Black bodies left in the street.
The warriors run rampant in times of need
Unable to see they hail from royalty.

Do you notice how closely your skin resembles gold?

GRAVITY

I lay here
As the fire burns
And takes my worries
I wonder if they become ashes or smoke
Either way I know they'll never reach the stars

I inhale the calmness
And exhale the chaos.
Men and women alike
have spent centuries
wishing to fly.
The weight we carry exceeds the strength of our
wings.
Gravity is constant.

the error in our ways

ABOUT THE WRITER

Eric Jordan Campbell is an Atlanta, Georgia based poet from Queens, New York who was born in 1992. His poetry travels the themes of love, miscommunication, mistreatment, loss, trauma, self love, healing, and existing on a background that is not meant for you to blend into. When Eric is not writing he is either experimenting with different art forms or performing spoken word and encouraging young writers to tell their stories.

Eric Jordan Campbell

the error in our ways

Made in United States
Orlando, FL
19 December 2023

41213279R00049